A Note to Parents and Teachers

Kids can imagine, kids can laugh and kids can learn to read with this exciting new series of first readers. Each book in the Kids Can Read series has been especially written, illustrated and designed for beginning readers. Funny, easy-to-read stories, appealing characters and topics, and engaging illustrations make for books that kids will want to read over and over again.

To make selecting a book easy for kids, parents and teachers, the Kids Can Read series offers three levels based on different reading abilities:

Level 1: Kids Can Start to Read

Short stories, simple sentences, easy vocabulary, lots of repetition and visual clues for kids just beginning to read.

Level 2: Kids Can Read with Help

Longer stories, varied sentences, increased vocabulary, some repetition and visual clues for kids who have some reading skills, but may need a little help.

Level 3: Kids Can Read Alone

Longer, more complex stories and sentences, more challenging vocabulary, language play, minimal repetition and visual clues for kids who are reading by themselves.

With the Kids Can Read series, kids can enter a new and exciting world of reading!

Pup and Hound
Catch a Thief

For Bill and Nancy, who still don't like cats! — S.H.

For Gus, who steals my lunch! — L.H.

Kids Can Read ® Kids Can Read is a registered trademark of Kids Can Press Ltd.

Text © 2007 Susan Hood
Illustrations © 2007 Linda Hendry

Kids Can Press acknowledges the financial support of the Government of Ontario, through the Ontario Media Development Corporation's Ontario Book Initiative; the Ontario Arts Council; the Canada Council for the Arts; and the Government of Canada, through the BPIDP, for our publishing activity.

Published in Canada by
Kids Can Press Ltd.
29 Birch Avenue
Toronto, ON M4V 1E2

Published in the U.S. by
Kids Can Press Ltd.
2250 Military Road
Tonawanda, NY 14150

www.kidscanpress.com

The artwork in this book was rendered in pencil crayon on a sienna colored pastel paper.
The text is set in Bookman.

Series editor: Tara Walker
Edited by Yvette Ghione
Printed and bound in Singapore

The hardcover edition of this book is smyth sewn casebound.

CM 07 0 9 8 7 6 5 4 3 2 1
CM PA 07 0 9 8 7 6 5 4 3 2 1

Library and Archives Canada Cataloguing in Publication

Hood, Susan
   Pup and hound catch a thief / Susan Hood ; illustrated by Linda Hendry.

(Kids Can read)
ISBN-13: 978-1-55337-972-0 (bound) ISBN-10: 1-55337-972-1 (bound)
ISBN-13: 978-1-55337-973-7 (pbk.) ISBN-10: 1-55337-973-X (pbk.)

1. Dogs—Juvenile fiction. I. Hendry, Linda II. Title. III. Series: Kids Can read (Toronto, Ont.)

PZ7.H758Puc 2006   j813'.54   C2006-902265-8

Kids Can Press is a *CORUS*™ Entertainment company

Pup and Hound
Catch a Thief

Written by Susan Hood

Illustrated by Linda Hendry

Kids Can Press

4

What was that?

Bang! Smash! Crash!

Cat dashed by,

spilling the trash.

Cat ran outside,

screeching "YE-OW!"

What was that

crazy Cat up to now?

Upstairs they found

the scene of the crime!

Who robbed the bank,

spilling nickels and dimes?

Hound puffed out his chest.

Pup made a gruff sound.

This was a job

for Pup and Hound!

They sniffed many smells,

hunting for clues.

The strongest smell

was a smell that Hound knew.

Who was the sneakiest

sneak on the farm?

Hound shook his jowls

and howled the alarm!

Hound tracked the smell

... and look at that!

The trail lead straight

to that sneaky Cat!

Cat climbed the tree

and leaped to the roof.

Aha! A cat burglar!

But Hound needed proof.

Pup and Hound spied on
Cat all that day.

But drat! All she did

was sleep and play.

Later that day,

geese honked in alarm.

Someone called "Help!"

across the farm.

Pup and Hound raced

over the lawn.

The farmer cried out.

Her locket was gone!

Bracelets were missing!

Her best earrings, too!

Cufflinks and hairpins ...

Oh, what should they do?

The family decided
to call the police.
The piglets agreed.
And so did the geese.

Hound sniffed around.

And who did he spy?

That sneaky old Cat

just slinking on by.

Hound followed Cat.

And Pup followed Hound.

They hid in a bush

when Cat turned around.

"Woof! Woof!" said Pup.

Look what he saw!

A twinkle ... a sparkle ...

He reached out his paw.

There in the nest

were earrings and rings!

The thief was a magpie

who loved shiny things!

"*Ah-ROOO!*" called Hound.

"*Ah-roo-roo!*" called Pup.

The farmers ran over.

The police car pulled up.

Good Pup! Good Hound!

They each got a bone.

But they wouldn't have found

the nest on their own.

Cat was no thief!

She was tracking the bird.

Case solved! Case closed.

Cat sat down and purred.

The bird never came back

to the house or the yard.

That bird wouldn't dare

with three friends on guard!